REMEMBRANCE

BOOK ONE: ARRIVAL

H. BUCHANAN

AUXmedia
Detroit, Michigan

REMEMBRANCE
Book One: ARRIVAL

Editor: Antoinette Gardner

Cover art: Jay Walsh

ISBN 978-0-9971996-9-7
LCCN 2016915977

AUXmedia, a division of Aquarius Press
www.remembranceproject.net

Printed in the United States of America

This book is dedicated to the memory of the Harlem Hellfighters, and to Maestro James Reese Europe.

You saved the world.

Cpl. David Pierce's Notebook
January 1, 1918

New Year's Day
(The 15th New York Arrives in France)

We marched off the boat with jazz,
les enfants perdu
            black orphans
rechristened
by the sea and the Holy Spirit
                                                            soldiers
advancing into the Kingdom.

This land will hear our song.

Part One: That Night

The French people knew no color line. All they seemed to want to know, that night, was that a great national holiday of their ally was being celebrated—and that made the celebration one of their own.

The spirit of emotional enthusiasm had got into the blood of our men; and they played as I had never heard them play before...

—*Capt. Maj. Arthur Little*
369th U.S. Infantry Regiment
Lincoln's Birthday Concert,
Opera House, Nantes, February 12, 1918

David's Letter to Giselle the Morning After the Blast

UNDELIVERED

February 13, 1918

I have nowhere to send this damn letter.

Where are you? All I can do is write this down because I can't speak fear into existence, not in the middle of a war. A fool, I write as if you can read this with your mind, some sort of mental telegraph, I guess. I wish. I didn't know you for long, but somehow, I know you.

We have returned to our base to receive orders. There will be no forgiveness for the attack last night. We will show the Germans who we are and why we're here.

Giselle, I pray that you survived. I swear I can feel you out there somewhere.

I will see you again.

Sincerely,
Cpl. David Pierce
93rd Division
369th U.S. Infantry Regiment
Old 15th New York

Cpl. James "Jimmy" Peyton's Journal
February 13, 1918

I'm starting this journal in hopes of writing a book about this war. If I survive, that is. Last night was incredible! Three amazing things happened, all at once:

1. Our band conquered France
2. I think David fell in love
3. We almost died in a German attack

Our concert drove those French folks crazy! I never felt more loved. The applause went on forever, and I felt so warm in there, like in a cocoon. I didn't want to leave. David was brilliant on his cornet solo, as always (I can only call him David in this journal, out in the real world he only wants to be called Pierce). He never shows his feelings, but even he got caught up in the excitement—I could tell.

We are soldiers newly arrived to save these people, but we are their musicians, too. When we're not in combat, our band tours the countryside to entertain the troops, the townsfolk, the wounded, and, well, the dead. This is just one part of a larger picture—many of us here signed up for this war because we believe in Lt. James Reese Europe's vision. He says our doing well over here will show the world the excellence of black men, and that will make things better for our people back home.

But back to last night. It took us a long time to get out of the opera house, because the townsfolk wanted to shake our black hands to thank us. Wow! We then get invited to this little club not too far away. It was cold outside, but we didn't care. The place had good food and drink. The music was nice, but so different from ours. First time seeing an accordion. The walls were painted red, and there were candles on each of the covered tables, so the room felt cozy. There was a step-up stage on the front right side of the room. The smiling and fluffy feathered showgirls had been dancing the *cancan* just before, and they were pretty, but you couldn't tell one from the other.

But this singer who came after them! Just lovely, with her soft eyes and smooth brown shoulders. Bare shoulders. Straps of sparkly blue and gold beads fastened at the back of her neck (like a swan's neck) barely held that silky, shapely dress up. Every man in the room wanted her, but we all knew we couldn't have her. Some things you just know. What impressed me most was her rich voice, singing those old sad French songs as if she'd lived each one. She and David stared at each other all night, and I knew something was happening. When her set was done, they just walked up to each other on the dance floor like it was old times.

After a while, David brought her over to our table. "*Bonjour, Mademoiselle,*" I said as I kissed her hand. I was showing off my new French. She was pleasant enough, but there was this watchfulness about her. They talked the rest of the night. I didn't eavesdrop, but I didn't need to—it was clear they were getting along fine.

I was getting up to give them some privacy when all of hell opened up right in front of us.

This French guy walked up, all proper. He was well dressed, but real stiff. He yanked up Giselle and ignored David. He told her it was time to leave.

Poor David! He looked confused, then angry as he sized up French Guy. When French Guy pulled on Giselle's arm again, David jumped to his feet. I jumped up too. My thinking was French Guy would have to get past the both of us.

But Giselle shocked us by suddenly walking off with French Guy. She didn't even look back. David tried to follow, but I pulled him back, thinking we didn't know what that story was. Just as I was about to say so, there was a huge BOOM! and everything went black.

When I opened my eyes, all I could see was darkness. I smelled smoke. I heard women screaming. All around us, feet were shuffling. I realized I was on the floor. David appeared above me, and he was shouting. I shouted back, "What?" because my ears were ringing. David cupped his hands around his mouth and shouted, "Blast!" I understood then. We were under attack.

As I started to rise, I heard the *tat-tat-tat* of machine guns.

"Down!" David shouted.

He shoved me back to the floor. We drew our pistols and dashed behind an overturned table to use it for cover. (We were trained how to take cover just the other day.)

I remember David shouting, "Two hostiles, 12 o'clock!"

I saw two Germans barging through the front doors. A classic sneak attack with an explosion, then follow-up with gunfire. (Just learned about that, too.) It dawned on me that they could kill every one of us in there.

Suddenly, David fired two quick shots at the men in the doorway, and they both went down. David is known as an expert shot. Hope I can get good one day soon—this was the first time in my life using a gun.

We scrambled to the front, careful to watch the door for more soldiers. Mostly everyone in the club had rushed to the back to hide under tables. David came face-to-face with one of our so-called fellow soldiers from the A.E.F. It was O'Dowd. We didn't like him—he didn't believe that Negroes should be serving in this war. O'Dowd had been shot. David asked him how bad he was hit. O'Dowd frowned and answered with, "Not bad, sorry to disappoint you." He was a smartass.

David said, "Yeah, I am disappointed, but even I won't leave you to the Krauts. Come on!" David lifted O'Dowd from the floor, supporting the big guy. I followed behind.

"Corporal Peyton!" David shouted.

"Yes sir!" I shouted back.

"We're getting out of here. Watch the door—it'll be like Leonidas and the 300."

"Huh?" I didn't know who that dude was, but we could have used 300 men at the time.

"We're shooting 'em as they come through that narrow-ass doorway!"

"Oh! Sir, yes sir!"

Just as I feared, two more pointy German helmets were rushing through the front door. We three opened fire, quickly taking them down. The other A.E.F. soldier who came with O'Dowd—Fitzgerald—made it to the door and was waiting for us, pistol drawn. Together, we American soldiers pressed forward through the door over the Germans' dead bodies and out into the dark night. I heard the sound of trucks pulling off. There was no sign of any other enemies nearby.

"A raid with civilians inside. Damn," David said with disgust.

"Yeah," Fitzgerald said. He grabbed O'Dowd from David and gave him a brief look of gratitude for saving his friend. We all knew the unity wouldn't last, but it felt good anyway. We four jumped into a Davidson-Cadillac armored car that was kept in town for emergencies. We sped back to the rail station so we could report on the attack.

That was my first encounter with the Germans, and I was still shaking after I was safely back at the base. David was quiet. Despite everything that happened, despite nearly losing his life in a flash, I knew his mind was on Giselle.

Giselle's Wire to David at Base 1, St. Nazaire
February 13, 1918

Corporal Pierce, I hope this note finds you well.

I received word from the mayor of Nantes that you left him a note inquiring after me. He is a friend, and he says to thank you again for the beautiful concert last night, it lifted his people's spirits. He also sends his regrets about what happened after.

I am relieved that you survived the raid. Your friend did as well?

I keep hearing about your band's excellence in every town. I am curious about this jazz you play.

Thank you for being concerned about me, but I am fine. I am putting this incident behind me, and you should do the same.

This is war, after all.

Best wishes for your band.

Sincerely,
Giselle

P.S. You are correct—Giselle is my stage name.

David's Reply to Giselle

UNDELIVERED

February 13, 1918

Giselle, I'm glad that you're okay. Thanks for the polite reply. However, I'm sure you'll agree you're being a little brief considering your first words to me were, "If you want to live, you need to leave this club. Now."

I remember the night very clearly. Just an hour before, our band brought down the house—the Nantes Opera House, for God's sake! Men in tuxedos cheering, women in evening gowns crying, French flags waving... There we were, a band from Harlem playing jazz, and these white folks were having a fit.

At the club I remember saying to you, "Say that again?" I was working on my next glass of cognac, so I was thinking maybe I hadn't heard you right. I was there to celebrate with my buddies. And then I saw you. Your band was playing pretty good, songbird. You were too bright for my eyes, though, all a-glitter in your gown, sparkling clips in your hair. What a beautiful voice you have.

Despite your warning, I wasn't going anywhere. Your eyes sparked when I defied your request—I think you liked that. We were comfortable, as if we'd done that dance before. You took my drink and studied me as you sipped, like you didn't know what to do with me. I took great delight in watching your red lips meet the rim of my glass.

You said I had to go, and I said something like, "If you're talking about those guys over there, I ain't worried about them." To make a point, I took back the glass and raised it at a couple of white soldiers from the A.E.F. sitting in a corner made extra dark just because they were sitting there. It's not enough we can't serve with them as fellow Americans—we can't be seen here either. They were furious that I was sitting there talking with you, but there was nothing they could do about it. They knew the minute they tried anything in that club, the French folks would take them down. The villagers adore the Black Watch.

You said it wasn't the soldiers, but you wanted to say more. Well, now's your chance. So many questions:

1. You are a black woman over here in France singing in French, so what's your story?

2. Who was that dude who interrupted us, the one you left with?

David's Wire to Giselle
February 14, 1918

Giselle, I'm glad you're okay.

Thanks for asking after the guy who was with me, Cpl. Peyton. He's just a kid from Detroit, but he likes to follow me around. I try to look out for him.

We have been touring by train through so many towns, playing in railway stations and public squares, including Angers, Tours, and Lyon. In Culoz, we put on a surprise concert for Maj. Gen. Kiernan, the commanding officer of the region, and he was impressed. We'll be stationed at the rest resort, Aix-les-Bains, for a couple of weeks. I hear that your band is on the way there, too.

I want to see you again.

In case you're wondering… No, I don't make a habit of writing letters to women I just met. One would think I'm busy enough trying to stay alive. But here we are. I'm reaching out to you for reasons I don't even know myself. We connected that night.

Please write back.

Sincerely,
David

David's Notebook
February 14, 1918

After this War

At the club, you graced us with a French soldier's tune. I could figure most of it out, because I know what a *Mademoiselle* is. I know about the townspeople crying a lot, *pleuré beaucoup*. I could see the tears in your eyes, too, as you sang this.

> *"Après la guerre fini*
> *Après les soldats anglais à gauche*
> *M'selle Frongsay pleuré beaucoup,*
> *Après la guerre fini."*
>
> *After the war ended*
> *After the English soldiers left*
> *Mademoiselle Frongsay cried a lot,*
> *After the war ended.*

Dearest Giselle, after this war ends, I will wipe away your tears, and you will see happiness.

I want that for you.

Field Marshall Eric von Helm's Wire to the German High Command
14 February 1918

Morning of 14 February 1918, plans for the Kaiser Battle underway.

Sturmtruppen raids have begun in French towns.

First miscommunication to Gen. Duchene, French Sixth Army, successfully delivered by the asset.

Note: Supplies running short. Early cases of influenza, extent among troops unknown. American divisions arriving to support Allies.

Repeat: The Americans have arrived.

Jimmy's Journal
February 14, 1918

Justice has been served. Just returned from my first raid. Intel from some local villagers gave us the location of the German raiding party that attacked the club. They were hiding just a few miles from the town in a worn down little house in the woods. They hadn't gotten far—I guess they were so arrogant they thought no one would find them.

We rode the train back to Nantes, then went the rest of the way on foot. Capt. Forbes led the raid, with Big Jim right behind him. David and I were behind Big Jim, followed by Fox and Grenade Tommy, two of our other guys. I had my pistol ready. Fox decided he would try out the bayonet contraption—we wished him luck with that.

Once we got to the farm, we spotted the house quickly in the bright moonlight. Everything was so still, one would never have guessed there were soldiers inside. The wait seemed like forever. Finally, there was some movement. A German soldier was scouting the perimeter. His helmet looked to be really tight-fitting, and that pointy tip looked peculiar. Once he rounded the corner of the house again and we were sure it was just him, Forbes signaled for Grenade Tommy to make his move. Grenade Tommy was so calm the entire time—I think he has killed people before. Funny, David was very calm, too...

Quickly, quietly, and with his blade drawn, Tommy rushed over and waited for the sentry to come round the back of the house again. When he did so, Tommy reached out and grabbed the sentry, who was startled. With one smooth move, Tommy slashed that guy's throat. I could hear him gurgle a little, then I saw black liquid spurting out down over his uniform. Tommy tossed him to the ground as if he were nothing and signaled to us.

Capt. Maj. Forbes ran up, and we were close behind. Once we reached the door, he signaled for Fox to kick it in. We rushed in. There was a man seated at a table. He appeared to be studying a map when we barged in. There was such a look of surprise on his face. The three Germans standing around him made to reach for their guns, but he stopped them with a raise of his hand.

"*Nein,*" he said. I knew that word. Sighing, he slowly rose and let Fox tie his arms around his back. The rest of us kept our pistols trained on the other three soldiers.

Capt. Maj. Forbes looked very pleased. "Well, men," he said. "You just captured your first Krauts."

Harlem Journal Interview with Percival "Fox" Fox,
Harlem Hellfighter
June 1, 1919

by Edwin Moore

[Excerpt reprinted from the May 1919 issue in honor of the late James Reese Europe, as our nation mourns the tragic loss of the great bandleader]

EM: Tell us more about James Reese Europe as you recall him. Would you say he was tough on you soldier-musicians?

Fox: Yes, you could say that, but he was very kind at the same time. There was so much at stake for us, so we welcomed his corrections at every turn. He had these knowing eyes that grabbed you, you couldn't escape his gaze if you wanted to. If those eyes were trained on you for a bad note you made, it was kind of spooky, so you didn't want that to happen. We all had so much to learn, not just about being soldiers, but there's always something new to learn about musicianship, even in the midst of war (laughs).

EM: The music was so different. Can you explain it?

Fox: It's kinda hard to put it into words, we just knew what to do. I will say I heard civilians describe our trumpets as talking trumpets. They could hear a *wah-wah* sound. (Laughs) some French musicians actually tried to search our horns! They thought there was some kind of hidden valves or something. Naw, it was just us making those sounds natural-like.

EM: You were taking a new sound to France, a sound they embraced as their own and never forgot.

Fox: That's right. I remember before we got there, Big Jim said I know there's a war going on, but this band is going to play in Paris. Sure as hell, we did.

Jimmy's Letter to His Sister
February 19, 1918

Hey, Sis!

I've been meaning to write sooner, but we're just getting the post running regular out here. Hope you and the kids are doing well. Well, we're finally here in France! I'll say it was a rough journey across the sea aboard the *Pocahontas*. We left mid-December and landed in Brest on New Year's Day. I was scared to disembark, but I was encouraged when the men started singing. The minute my feet touched land, a sergeant grabbed me and asked if I could bugle. I told him yeah, then he told me I was now chief bugler of the Company and a corporal (but I later found out I'm still being paid as a private).

We call this icy winterland Valley Forge. We are short on food and clothing, and there was no heat in those railway cars. Our camp is in St. Nazaire. At first, instead of training us like real soldiers, they just had us digging ditches, laying tracks and removing unexploded shells from the fields. But that's no surprise, really—we just brought an old war to a new country, unfortunately. White Marines in other units have been killing black soldiers, but the 15th New York is fighting back. From now on, one white soldier is dropping for every black one. Word has it that General Pershing was pressured by somebody (the NAACP?) to get us out of here fast. We're here to fight, not lay railroad tracks. We'll soon be headed to the Front, to Chalôns. We are the first regiment ever known to turn in its military equipment and train with French machine guns, automatics, and grenades. (Turns out the French rifles are only good for holding bayonets.)

We were also given gas masks and advised to grab the masks off of any dead Germans we come across.

I wonder why we need gas masks?

Well, anyhow, your big brother is going to save the world! I'll ship the kids something soon as I get a chance to visit one of these towns again.

Luv ya,
Jimmy

Amie Leduc's Letter to Her Aunt
February 20, 1918

Tante Liliane,

I hope you are well. I am doing well. Mlle. Giselle tells me I am doing a good job. I am having the best time helping her choose her gowns for her shows. We look through the *Callot Souers* catalogs for the coming season's fashions. Would you believe that girdles are going out of style? I know that you will never give up yours (smile).

Mlle. has been kind enough to give me some of her dresses (where will I, a country girl, ever wear them?) and she even showed me how to make a nice *chignon* for myself using mirrors. She says my hair is pretty, so I should take care of it. She has given me some of her fine soaps. Lilac soap from the south of France from one of her admirers, what a luxury! I will be sending you some of it, too, when I go to the post for her again. She sends me to the post quite frequently, now that I think of it.

A secret between you and me—Mlle. likes someone. I saw him at the club after the concert. Mlle. sent me back to the hotel early. I could not help but smile, because I have never seen her look at a man in such a way. He is *negre*, but he's tall and handsome, and he only had eyes for her. I am young, but I know love when I see it.

As for her manager, M. Thierry—he may love her, too, I think. But he is not a good man. There is something cold about him.

He does not notice me much, but I do my best to stay out of his way. He smokes and studies maps of our country, despite having lived here all of his life. He has a strange way of talking, always addressing his fellow Frenchmen formally, especially so-called friends who visit. They all appear to have a lot on their minds. They do not smile or laugh.

I do hope M. Soldier Pierce will come by soon—she looked so happy with him that night.

Love and Flowers,
Amie

Giselle's Letter to David
February 20, 1918

David,

I realize that my reply to your letter was quite brief. I have my reasons, the main one being I do not want to encourage anything. Like yourself, I am busy with my own tour. I am not looking to make new friends just now. I will admit I enjoyed talking with you very much. We live in dangerous times, and connecting with kindred spirits gets us through the rough times.

I did not mean to alarm you at the club. Again, I apologize for any misunderstanding. There were rumors about Germans roaming the village, and we were advised to be watchful. I have since learned you belong to the Black Watch, so there is no need to worry about you at all—you have come here to save the French people.

As for your compliments, *merci beaucoup*. I am just a girl who enjoys singing, nothing special about me. That gentleman you saw is my manager, Thierry. He was simply reminding me of the late hour.

It is very exciting to hear about your tour of the countryside. I know that your band is lifting people's spirits.

I do not doubt your sincerity in reaching out to me. I can tell you are an honorable man. I will be honest with you and say that I, too, felt something, a connection. But it was just a fleeting moment at the end of a very long night. The war will be over soon enough, and you will be on your way back home to the United States.

Again, it was a pleasure meeting you. Stay safe.

Sincerely,
Giselle

Harlem Journal Interview with Noble Sissle,
15th Infantry Regimental Band
Edwin Moore, Reporting
February 21, 1918

A Special Report on "Harlem's Own" from the Battlefield
by Edwin Moore

EM: Tell me about that night at the Opera House in Nantes. Is it safe to assume this was the night James Reese Europe's band took France by storm?

Sissle: You could say that. Colonel Hayward has brought his band over here and started ragitimitis in France; ain't this an awful thing to visit upon a nation with so many burdens? But when the band had finished and people were roaring with laughter, their faces wreathed in smiles, I was forced to say that this is just what France needs at this critical time.

EM: After a French march, the second part of the program opened with Sousa's "Stars and Stripes Forever," correct?

Sissle: Yes, and before the last note of the martial ending had been finished the house was ringing with applause.

EM: Next followed an arrangement of Southern melodies...

Sissle: Plantation melodies... And then came the fireworks, "The Memphis Blues." Big Jim's baton came down with a soul-rousing crash of cymbals.

EM: It was described that following Europe's lead, the musicians relaxed their stiff military demeanor, half-closed their eyes, and seemed to forget their surroundings. The cornet and clarinet players began to manipulate notes in a different way.

Sissle: In that typical rhythm which no artist has ever been able to put down on paper. The drummers hit their stride with shoulders shaking in syncopated time, and Europe turned to the trombones who sat patiently waiting for their cue to have a jazz spasm. The jazz germ hit the audience and they were moving like they do in America, as an eagle rocking it...

David's Notebook
February 22, 1918

Tracks

We are their miracle,
brown angels with trumpets and cymbals,
a Heavenly Host dispatched from another god.

We are their shame,
frozen spirits rumbling on trains,
a Brittle Winged pledged to barren Golgotha.

Jimmy's Journal
February 22, 1918

Early morning here at the base in St. Nazaire, over an hour's journey by train from Nantes. We stood at attention for what felt like hours. Capt. Majors Forbes and Little, Capt. Fish (we call him Ham Fish), and Lt. Europe were addressing us. Capt. Maj. Forbes really believes in us, especially David. They are friends from way back. I saw them in action during one of those nasty brawls we had back in the States—the white soldiers really gave us a hard time at those training camps. Forbes looks out for David, and they fight side by side on the battlefield.

"Soldiers, you just got your first taste of the German Spring Offensive!" Forbes said. "These bastards have some devious plans for this country. It's up to us to stop them." Despite the thick greenery of the woods, little patches of early sunlight pushed through to shine on his fiery hair. "We're gonna keep hitting right back, and hard! Aren't we, men?"

I heard some early morning mumbles of "yeah" throughout the crowd. David looked terrible. I knew he hadn't gotten his morning smoke or a hot cup of coffee yet, but it was more than that. He was clenching a crumpled note in one hand. Odds were it was from Giselle.

Clearly not happy with the dull response from his half-awake soldiers, Lt. Europe stepped forward. He barked, "Atten-HUT!" and all our eyes were upon our leader, that great man.

"I don't think Capt. Maj. heard you all too well," Lt. Europe said softly. His eyes were calm behind his glasses, but he was to be obeyed.

"Sir, yes sir!" we all shouted as one.

"The Germans have seen fit to attack known civilian targets," he continued. "We have to show them who's boss. We have intel on one of their main outposts, just about two hours from here. Our orders are to take the outpost. Are you with me, men?"

"Sir, yes sir!"

"Captain Fish here will organize the squads, so listen out for your assignments. Dismissed!" Captains Maj. Little and Forbes walked off to the command tent. Armed soldiers that were guarding the entrance moved aside to allow him inside.

When I looked back at David, he had finally found a moment to light his cigarette. I rushed up to greet him. He looked like he needed some cheer.

"Fine weather we're having for a raid," I said.

"Yeah," was all he said.

I asked him if he was still thinking about the other night. I knew he knew what I meant.

"Not at all," David said.

"She was something special," I pressed. "You know, our telegraph and post runs pretty fast out here now. Why don't you drop her a line? Some of the locals will do courier runs for a few *francs*," I added. He looked at me, but I couldn't tell if he was mad or not. I didn't care if I was hitting a trip wire. He's been a different person, and it has everything to do with her. There's a new energy about him, as if a light has been turned on. That has to mean something.

After a time, he said, "What in God's name are you talking about?"

"It was nice to see a little fire in your eyes for a change. Sometimes you so cool, I wonder if you dead," I said. "But the minute you saw her… *whoo-ee*!"

David took a long drag of his cigarette then said, "Kiddo, I don't know what you're talking about, but I'm kindly going to ask you to fuck off right about now."

Then up walked Preach, our chaplain. He's in the Word of course, but he drinks and gambles with us all the time.

He always starts with, "Soldiers… Men of Bronze! Men of God! Now don't ya'll be spending time in them dance halls. That would break ya'll mamas' hearts!" Preach was a youngish man from Harlem like David, but he had an old man's way about himself. "There'll be no talk of death before we enter into battle tonight!"

I kept pressing my luck with David. I said, "Preach, can you tell David here about the wages of sin? You see, he's been contemplating sinning with a French woman back in that town." David gave me a "I'm gonna kick your ass" look. "What you think about that, Preach?" I was enjoying it too much.

Preach said, "Well, lemme see." He put his hand on his chin, thinking. "First thing I wanna know is… is she pretty?"

"She's beautiful, Preach. She black… but she French, too, ain't that something?" I added.

"Then in that case, David my son… you gon' and git that girl, the Lord will forgive ya!" Preach cackled and gave David a little shove. David shoved back, but Preach stayed cool. David then took a deep breath to calm himself.

"Preach, you lucky you got the Lord on your side," David said, "or my boot would be on your neck right now." He used his boot to ground out his unfinished cigarette instead, then he walked off.

David is mad right now, but I know he'll let me catch up with him later.

David's Letter to Sgt. Willard Toussaint, Retired
February 23, 1918

Quiet around here since the raids. The Germans we caught are now prisoners—chained at the ankles, they do hard labor around the camp. It's strange watching them do the work we brothers had to do just months before. Stripped of their spinning shells and arrogance, the Germans look almost pitiful in their prisoner uniforms. I'm starting to think that a lot of them really don't want this war, just like when you and me were in the thick of it back then. Of course there's the vicious bunch who enjoy fighting, but I'm seeing a lot of regular men who look tired and confused most of the time. Many of the prisoners have been friendly with us here, but we have to be cautious in case it's a trick.

Rehearsal this morning. Big Jim pulled me aside, said he's planning an all-Negro orchestra to tour the States when we get back, wants me to join up. Told him I'd think about it—I'm supposed to be in touch with Ruth about inquiring after that Harlem nightclub we might be able to buy. Strange to go back to working on songs after running around in the dark with weapons ready to kill somebody. We musicians kill, then we heal, I guess. Just hope the killing doesn't become the only thing.

There's a comfort in warming up on scales and runs—you can always count on them to be the same every time and they always get you to a good place. I am worried about this damp cold rusting out this old cornet, but Command is doing its best to keep our instruments dry and air-tight in the musicians' tent. Sissle moans every day about how he shouldn't have brought his own personal violin over here. This air is terrible for the wood. The days he can't play because we're on the march, he says his violin suffers. He says our instruments are a part of us, and they suffer when we don't play them. My cornet has suffered because I really haven't been playing it with my whole self since I re-upped. My old teacher in Harlem would say something's on my mind that I haven't made crystal yet.

I met someone the other night, and I'm trying to find her again, but we're heading out soon—I'm running out of time. She is a wonderful singer.

Enough about me. Hope things are well with Daisy, tell her I said hello. Will write again soon.

Yours in the Fight,
David

Jimmy's Journal
February 23, 1918

It's great here in Aix-les-Bains!

We get hot water baths, nice shaves, clean haircuts. This was a former health resort, ruins from the Roman Empire, I hear. Our primary assignment is to provide entertainment for the American troops, but it's been fun playing for the civilians, because they appreciate us so much. Command has told us we are going where no other American soldiers have stepped foot. We are on a mission of great importance. We are not merely musician-soldiers of the American Army, but ambassadors from America. We all take that very seriously. This is our chance to show the world who we are, so we're working hard.

Rehearsals in the mornings, and concerts in the afternoons and evenings. Most of the concerts are held in the Casino, a 1,000 seat theater, but we play in the parks on Tuesdays and Fridays. We've also played at Chambéry, an old cathedral city not far from here, for church services. It's a beautiful place and also the former home of philosopher Jean Jacques Rousseau, another dude I have to learn about.

We've done so well here, our stay has been extended about ten more days! I know that David will be relieved to hear it. He's been roaming back and forth looking for Giselle, as her band is supposed to be here, too.

HEADQUARTERS, 369TH INFANTRY
AMERICAN EXPEDITIONARY FORCES
23 February 1918

MEMORANDUM:

1. Issue reminder to troops the penalties for the following:

   Striking an Officer: IMPRISONMENT

   Desertion: PUNISHABLE BY DEATH

BY ORDER OF LIEUT. COL. SHANE LEWIS

Copy to Cpt. Maj. Forbes

David's Note to Giselle's Hotel Room

<u>DELIVERED BY MESSENGER</u>

February 23, 1918

I knew I'd see you again.

I'm not one for believing in fate, but here we are. When I saw you sitting in the garden near the fountain in Aix-les-Bains this morning, it was out of a dream. Just like in that dream, you were waiting for me. It was cold today, but the way the sun seemed to shine only on you, it looked like a page out of a book of fairytales. You greeted me with such a beautiful smile.

It's only right that we're put here together. It's a wonderful place, a temporary escape from this war. Soldiers come here to recuperate, and we entertain them. We're both doing a good thing, using music to lift their spirits, to heal them.

I'll see you this evening at the Casino.

It will be a Battle of the Bands, *oui*?

D

Giselle's Letter to David
<u>DELIVERED BY MESSENGER</u>
February 25, 1918

David, thank you for these lovely evenings. I enjoy our walks after the concerts, even in the chilly air. The moon seems brighter when I'm with you. I like knowing that you enjoy many of the same things—good books, art, and all kinds of music. If not for the bombings, I would be happy to show you the Louvre in Paris.

Thank you for the compliments on my band, but let me speak about your own band. *Magnifique*!

I counted at least forty players! Yours is the first foreign band to play *La Marseillaise* so well! I heard that when you performed it at the opera house, it took the audience twelve bars before they recognized their own song. Those dancing songs, they are the jazz, *oui*? You keep everyone dancing!

I want to know more about this jazz. I accept your invitation to dinner.

Giselle

P.S. *Mais non*, I will not be telling you my real name. You will have to keep guessing (smile).

David's Note to Giselle

LEFT AT THE DESK OF GISELLE'S HOTEL

February 26, 1918

When can I see you again? I wake up to find you gone. Where could you have gotten to so quickly? The sun is still long to arrive. I'm writing you by moonlight.

I realize I don't even know where you live when you're not on tour. And what regiment is your band attached to?

Do you have a home in Montmartre? My friend Willard lives there.

I'll wait out front for you, but I have to report back to camp by breakfast.

D

Jimmy's Journal
February 26, 1918

David was late to camp this morning. He missed stand-to on the fire step, stand-down at sunup, reveille and breakfast. Lucky for him, there was no sunrise attack waiting for him. At least not from the enemy, that is.

Capt. Maj. Forbes was furious. He marched David straight into his tent but they weren't there very long. When they came back out, Capt. Maj.'s face was still red.

After training, I brought David leftover tea and *baguettes* some villagers had risked to bring us. I apologized about the tea being cooled by the chilly air and all.

"Well, thanks, kiddo," was all he said. He was down and I knew it had to do with Giselle. I wanted to ask so badly, but David gave me a warning look. He started walking, and I followed.

"Come on, we've got rehearsal."

David's Notebook
February 26, 1918

Reveille

Atten-hut, soldier!

Feel the cold sun's
fresh anointing
as it singes
your shaved skull
brands your mind
with your mission:

Fight for them.
Fight for
US.

Giselle's Note to David at the Base
February 27, 1918

David, I am sorry that I left you without saying goodbye.

That night was special, but it was a mistake.

You are tempting me to become an even greater sinner than I already am. I would only cause you pain. There are things you do not know that would change your opinion of me. I could not bear it.

Forget about me.

G

David's Letter to Giselle
February 27, 1918

Dearest Giselle,

From one sinner to another, there is absolutely nothing—I mean nothing—that could change my opinion of you.

So much has already been said between us without words. With you, I can be my true self, and I saw glimpses of your true self. You are a good person, no matter what you say.

I'm no fool. I know that we're residents in Hell right now, but I think we can climb up out of here together.

Don't give up on us. We've just begun.

D

Part Two: Dark Spring

Patience, then, without compromise; silence without surrender; grim determination never to cease striving until we can vote, travel, learn, work and enjoy peace—all this, and yet with it and above it all the tramp of our armies over the blood-stained lilies of France to show the world again what the loyalty and bravery of black men means.

—***W.E.B. DuBois**, The Crisis*

Jimmy's Journal
March 17, 1918

It was hard to leave the peaceful Aix-les-Bains. We are now headed to war. Up till now, there were only stories told second-hand from soldiers who survived the Front—now it's our turn to gulp down this sour red wine. I'm hearing that the Germans like to crucify captured soldiers, and they really like to slit throats.

And now I know why we need gas masks.

From this train's window, all I see is destruction for miles on end—entire villages hollowed out. Farmland burned to a crisp. Long strips of barbed wire stretched out for miles. I see thousands of little crosses and flags marking the graves of both French and German soldiers. They will sleep in eternity all mixed in together. No nations, just souls.

Where does the music fit into this story now?

The Front was covered with these deep narrow trenches carved into the earth, surrounded by countless rows of barbed wire... Something made me stop for a moment, and sure as God is my witness a German mortar landed atop a soldier just ahead of me, and then he was no more...

—***Recollections of Capt. Maj. Forbes*** *on the 369th's First Artillery Casualties on the Five-Mile Hike to the Front*

HEADQUARTERS, 369TH INFANTRY
AMERICAN EXPEDITIONARY FORCES

FIELD NOTE

NOTHING is to be written on this side except the date and signature of the sender. Sentences not required may be erased. <u>If anything else is added the post card will be destroyed.</u>

__I am quite well.

__I have been admitted into hospital
__sick and am going on well.
__wounded and hope to be discharged soon.

__I am being sent down to the base.

__I have received your
letter dated________________.
telegram dated______________.
parcel dated________________.

Letter follows at first opportunity.

I have received no letter from you
__lately.
__for a long time.

Signature only___________________________
Date___________

Philip Pierce's Letter to David at the Base
February 15, 1918
RECEIVED LATE MARCH

Brother, received your letter, glad to know you made it there okay. You saw fit to return to France so quickly, but it was nice having you around here again. I understand, though, especially after what happened to Mitch. Everybody's looking out for his wife and kids now, but they need you, too. We all lean on your strength, myself included. But after what you did for me, I have no right to ask anything more of you.

We'll talk when you return home. I want to make things right, just give me a chance. Till then, I'll keep the dust off of all your books here, Shakespeare.

You're living the dream, crossing the ocean and shooting up Germans like a real hero. Proud of you.

Stay safe.
Phil

HEADQUARTERS, 369TH INFANTRY
AMERICAN EXPEDITIONARY FORCES
28 February 1918

MEMORANDUM:

1. Issue Reminder on How to Attack Enemy's Line:

Begin attack with heavy preliminary bombardment of the enemy lines

Gather the troops for the attack quietly and discreetly

Send troops over the top at a precise time. Tell them to walk, not run. Proceed forward at a steady pace to ensure entire attacking line arrives together with maximum impact

Use gas to cover your attack, but make sure wind isn't blowing gas back

As soon as objective has been taken, send the second wave in fast

BY ORDER OF LIEUT. COL. SHANE LEWIS

Copy to Cpt. Maj. Forbes

Amie Leduc's Letter to Her Aunt
March 20, 1918

Dearest *Tante* Liliane,

It is my prayer you are safe. We have heard that the Germans have reached our village. How I long to sit at your feet as you knit, humming. I miss your onion soup with the creamy cheese on top.

I know that you want me to always be your cheerful girl, so I will do my best and write to you as if nothing has changed.

Mlle. Giselle's band will be performing at the *Opéra de Paris*! I have been hard at work making her gowns. We had hoped to order something new from the Madeleine Vionnet collection, but there is no time, and we don't know how badly the post is being affected by the war.

She has been sad lately. When M. Thierry left, he was angry with her. He grabbed and shook her and said something about the importance of their work, but she shoved him away. I don't know where M. Soldier Pierce is, but I hope he will come back.

Love and Flowers,
Amie

Jimmy's Journal
March 21, 1918

David is the best soldier in this war, because he doesn't give up. I know this because of his relentless pursuit of the beautiful Giselle. For weeks, he has been volunteering to assist with supply and mail runs from camp to camp throughout the countryside, so it gives him the opportunity to stop in these little towns and ask questions. He tries to ditch me, but I know he needs me. Even Capt. Maj. Forbes knows it—he looks the other way and lets me go after him.

When we first met at training camp, I was a seventeen-year-old kid who knew nothing and nobody. I had never been away from home before. I was starting to regret my decision to join up, especially after running into trouble with Lil' Chuck, who was not little at all. Lil' Chuck was a giant, bald, meat-headed Negro from New Jersey who didn't like New Yorkers. He had been in previous showdowns with his fellow soldiers a few times before. I didn't understand why he couldn't see the big picture and realize we're going to be just Americans over here. Because he had seen me standing next to David, he assumed I was from New York, too.

Lil' Chuck shoved me.

I told him, "Hey, I got no trouble with you, man. I'm from Detroit. You know, we build the motor cars?"

Lil' Chuck told me to shut up.

"The kid ain't from New York. Leave him alone," David calmly told him. He had been leaning against the wall in the train station, smoking. We had just finished our first rehearsal as a regimental band. (I was so glad I had let the recruiters know I could play an instrument! I was kind of skinny and didn't want to be assigned to kitchen duty or something worse.) David was an experienced soldier, having served with the famous Willard Touissant in the French Foreign Legion, then the French flying corps. Touissant went on to the elite Lafayette Escadrille, but I don't know what David was doing by that point. Word was he was promoted to Sergeant but was busted down for some reason. They left the Air Corps, with Touissant staying in France and David returning home. David later re-upped to serve over here again (for reasons I'll probably never understand). In our band, David is the lead cornetist, and after hearing him play, that is justified.

"Aww, what, this your girlfriend?" Lil' Chuck said, taunting.

Somebody in the background said, "Chuck, you don't want to do that."

Chuck smirked as he eyed David. I could tell that he was used to pushing folks around.

Slowly, David took one last drag of his cigarette and then put it out on the concrete floor with his boot. He stepped up into Lil' Chuck's face. David told me he'd been in his fair share of street fights in Harlem running with his brother. Too bad Lil' Chuck didn't know that.

"Whatcha gon' do—" was all Lil' Chuck said before he got his lights punched out. He hit the floor with a thud. We called

Lil' Chuck a "Lil' punk" from then on, and there was no more trouble.

From that moment on, I've been David's right hand. I want to know everything about this two-sided man, the great musician and the cold soldier. I know he can teach me a thing or two. I'm in step with him, and he never tells me to fuck off.

Except for that one time I said what I said about Giselle back in St. Nazaire.

The Stormtroopers took everything from us, our food and supplies, leaving us with nothing. They did not care if we lived or died. My parents were too weary to fight anymore, Papa having deserted the army. We lived in shame because of that, but we were grateful to have him back home with us. The German onslaught was overwhelming, reducing our village to dust. The children in town were still expected to attend school on days when there was no bombing. We were taught to no longer say, "*Maman,*" but the harsh "*Mutter,*" words to prepare us for our German future. We were always reminded how lucky we were that the soldiers let us live. On the day the troopers looted our house, I got angry and shouted, "The Black Watch is coming. *Vous chiennes!*" The soldier looked scared for a minute. He shoved his rifle in my face. Then, he simply grinned and knocked me to the floor. He said the Fatherland will crush those *negers* and cut off their tails.

—***Recollections of Emile Forte, Survivor***
St. Michael Offensive, Spring 1918

Giselle's Letter to David at the Base
March 22, 1918

David, it would mean very much to me if this letter finds you alive. After we left Aix-les-Bains, we heard your unit had been assigned to the Front. I did not know that the bandmembers would be placed in the most dangerous zone. But you are soldiers first. Our own band is stationed near Chalôns to perform at a hospital there. We are not far apart, but the war keeps us miles apart.

I regret leaving you that morning.

I miss you, and I accept your offer of redemption. I will not promise you anything, but I would like to try. Let me know when you can get leave, and I will meet you. Anywhere.

Stay safe,
G

Giselle's Songbook
March 22, 1918

That Night

That night,
the moon was shining bright.
That night,
we forgot the strife.

Who could ever believe
two friends, *deux bon amis*

Could fall so fast—
Can this real-ly last?

That night,
the war came to an end.
That night,
our lives began again.

Can this really be?
True love, *mon cheri*?

The world was ours,

that night.

This was our day! I commanded my men to attack the enemy lines with a mixture of bloodthirstiness and rage. It was cold, so I was wearing my heavier leather coat with the fur collar. I lit a last cigarette that I had been holding onto. I felt the need to kill. When the barrage ended, we made our move, jumping down into the trench. I quickly turned a corner in the winding trench's wooden plank floors, pistol at the ready. I came across a wounded English soldier on the floor. He was shivering and calling out to God. He held up a family photograph and pleaded for mercy. He was a coward. I put my pistol to his muddy face and pulled the trigger.

—***Recollections of Klaus Yaeger,***
23-year-old Hero of Operation Mihiel:
The Youngest Commander to Rise to Lieutenant
and Command Stormtroopers

The battle is won, the English have been utterly defeated.

—Georg Alexander von Müller's Diary Entry
After the First German Successes of the Spring Offensive
23 March 1918

David's Letter to Giselle's Hotel in Chalôns
March 30, 1918

It's probably shell-shock, but I think I just received your letter. If I did, then I am overjoyed. If I didn't, I'll just pretend that I did. War shows us what is real, removing the veil of so-called civilized understandings. Everything else is an illusion.

I choose to believe you are real. You will be a slow burning flare guiding me through this underworld.

D

Preach's Sermon Notes
March 30, 1918

Heavenly Father, it appears our regiment is now continuously in need of your grace. We thank you for the sacrifice for our sins that has already been paid on the Cross. We humbly ask that you accept the souls of our fellow soldiers who have stepped off into Glory.

Amen

In the notes' margins: Father, I'm afraid to ask why this is happening.

Jimmy's Journal
March 30, 1918

So this is what hell looks like. I can't get over the planning of these trenches, long open coffins dug deep into the earth. Mounds of dirt and sand bags piled up around our heads, crowned with rusting barbed wire. After a five-mile march here across open farmland and flat fields, we had to practically dive to get down in here. Nobody stops shooting because you're moving into your new digs.

I was warned to not let my feet get wet, but that's already happening. The spring rains are making muddy little rivers down in here. Gangrene is the biggest enemy outside of the exploding Jack Johnsons, the bullets, and the rats, who grow fat from human meat. We've already experienced some intense *barrages* already, and I've seen dead bodies sitting in the trenches with their fellow living soldiers because there's no time for burials. The French government only allows captains and above to be buried, and most families are too poor to take home the bodies, and that's only if we can get them out of here first. We wear identity tags, but if we're killed, tags won't do us much good. I keep hearing about this mysterious figure all in white who appears on the battlefield to tend to the wounded, but he never gets hit. Some think it might be the Lord. I don't know, but if it is Him, I hope He comes back.

We guard our trench, the Valley of Death, in threes: front, support, reserve. Good things come in threes, right? The artillery officer stationed at forward observing has the most dangerous job. Most times they put me at rear, supervising the ammo and supplies. I think they do this because I am one of the youngest. At night, searchlights guard against night attacks. The noise is a constant drone in my ears, so you really can't hear anybody without shouting. We have signalers who use Morse code or semaphore flags. Runners get messages to and fro, risking their lives every time.

Most of the time, we read books and throw hand grenades. I'm determined to keep up with my journal. I'm hoping to be able to read this all again one day as an old man.

David warns me against my rifle getting jammed with mud, as we're short on cleaning oil. Some of these cats have made their trenches pretty homey, hanging pictures and making their own charcoal to cook with. I hear the German trenches have shelving.

So, now all I think about is what one of those four Davis brothers from the Bronx in New York said to me at training camp: "To be somebody you had to belong to the 15th Infantry or jealously look at them in uniform."

Ha.

Men are not often visible in modern war, because to make any show at all against the infernal machinations of Messrs. Krupp, Schneider, Creuset and Co., they must bury themselves in the earth, and only rise up to shoot if their enemy is sufficiently foolhardy as to show himself.

—***Ashmead Bartlett***, *Daily Telegraph*

David's Notebook
April 1, 1918

Landmine Blues

Buried my brother down low,
low into tha ground.

Buried my brother down low,
low into tha ground.

Said my prayers for his soul—
took…
his…
pistol…
for my own…

Brother told me one mornin', said
"Well, my time is nigh."

Brother told me one mornin', said
"Well, my time is nigh."

"Can't keep dodging these mines…
my…
sweet…
widow's…
gonna cry…"

Buried my brother down low,
low into tha ground.

Buried my brother down low,
low into tha ground.

Said my prayers for his soul—
took...
his...
pistol...
for my own...

David's Letter to Willard
April 5, 1918

Willard, I should have taken your advice and not re-upped. How I envy you now, sitting back in your cozy home, drinking the finest wine and reminiscing while I shiver out here in the cold mud, trying to bum a light.

On break from the trenches, headed for a new sector tomorrow. They have me training some of the youngsters in French-style combat, which I know so well from my time with you. A new way of fighting as a regiment. We exchanged our Springfields for Lebel rifles with long blades. We practice fencing with dummies every morning. I've been helping the instructor because of the language barrier between him and these kids. He is impressed with our unit's skills, both hand-to-hand and bayonet. I told him that thanks to boxing, the feint, thrust, and parry are basically the same idea. He then said, "Boxing? Jack Johnson!" and started to do a boxer's shuffle, but he was so tall and skinny, he looked absolutely ridiculous. We all laughed our asses off. The cats who play baseball back home can throw grenades farther than the French soldiers, too, so these instructors are absolutely in love with us.

Got this kid following me around, Jimmy Peyton. Reminds me of when I used to follow you, so I guess it's my turn to be the big brother. He's from Detroit, got this "let's get to it" way about himself, which can be annoying and funny at the same time. He doesn't know when to keep his mouth shut, but sometimes he says something real deep.

Peyton constantly comments on the weather, though. What weather should we discuss over here? The overcast skies streaked blacky-red from the bombings, or the hot splash of blood across our cheeks in the icy wind when we are dumb enough to raise our heads from the trench at the wrong moment? Yeah, once he's been down deep in here for a while, Peyton won't have much to say about that.

How goes plans for the club? I'm still thinking about your offer. My own house band… If I can live to see 26, maybe so. But you might get tired of me hanging around. There's more to tell you about that singer here, you've probably heard of her. Giselle, with the Bon Nuit Band? I'm going to tell her about your club idea.

Well, friend, this is the war we feared would be coming. We're hearing thousands are dropping by the day. The "rules" of civilized fighting are being broken. It's not enough to just shoot a man anymore, or fight him hand-to-hand. Now we have rolling canons, long-range artillery, grenade launchers, flying machines that kill. We're wiping out entire villages. No nation will emerge from this war with clean hands. God is going to make us pay, as if us black folks haven't paid enough already. We came here for noble reasons, but we're a part of this now.

Forbes is still as ambitious as ever, wants to make us the stars of the show, and I don't mean musically. We have an excellent unit, everybody's giving their all. It looks like Command is pleased with our efforts thus far, and Gen. Gouraud (we call him Pa Gouraud) has praised our men, so maybe something good will come from this.

Taking an overnight train ride to the advanced zone—as you know, I can't give you specifics, but you know what I'm saying. More trenches. The tough part begins.

You better be taking good care of Daisy. How did the paint job turn out?

Yours in the Fight,
David

When we awoke and got off the train, we suddenly heard a shriek through the air like the screaming of a pheasant, followed by a tremendous explosion of a large shell from the German line. Turns out I and about half of the band members were mistakenly placed on a troop car that was headed directly for the Front. It took us two days to find our way back to Givry-en-Argonne and the 369th's camp.

—Noble Sissle, Memoirs, 131

James Reese Europe's Reply to Eubie Blake
April 9, 1918

If you think of the comforts you are having over there and think of the hardships we are having over here, you'd be happy I am sure to go on "suffering"... I have some wonderful opportunities for you to make all the money you need. Eubie, the thing to do is to build for the future, and build securely and that is what I am doing.

When I go up I will take you with me.

You can be sure of that.

David's Note to Giselle from the Trenches
Date Unknown

The way I see it now, there is no "before" anymore—

there's only the "after," starting with the moment
I first held you.

That's the only way I'm keeping time from now on…

David's Note to Giselle from the Trenches
Date Unknown

i surrender to you only.

i lay down my shield

my sword

my rifle

my cross.

David's Note to Giselle from the Trenches
Date Unknown

Joy

The joy you give me will never be written about.

It refuses to be trapped on a page.

I wear it as my armor.

David's Note to Giselle from the Trenches
Date Unknown

Your body is a temple of blinding white fire.
That night, I became your phoenix.

What fool willingly allows himself to be consumed in your scorching death-life?

'Tis I.

Such madness, but by God, I love it…

Giselle's Letter to David in the Trenches

<u>DELIVERED BY MESSENGER</u>

April 10, 1918

David, your notes are making me blush. I feel so guilty that some young runner is out there dodging mortars and bullets just so you can tell me what you want to do with me when you get back to the countryside! You keep saying that's their job, but if they only knew what messages they are carrying (wink).

Yes, I know Montmartre well. Our band plays there. There is a street where you will feel right at home, where I have heard about other musicians like yourself. It's called *rue de Clichy*. There is a drummer there, Louis Mitchell, who is looking for musicians. He has plans for a club.

To finally answer the question you keep asking, I have been singing since I was a little girl. My parents are musicians and were on tour here. My mother, an opera singer from Virginia, taught me how to sing. France has been good to our musicians, *oui*?

What is your family like? Do you have a sister? Brother? Are they as bold as you?

I find myself praying for you every day now.

G

David's Notebook
April 13, 1918

Spirituelle

Walk now, with me
down *rue de Clichy*
walk now, with me
down *rue de Clichy*
walk now, with me
down *rue de Clichy*.

Leave your cares in dat ole world . . .

Come live and be free . . .

Your father say, "You cannot leave, your soul is anchored here—
to the fields
to the streets
to all that you hold dear."

I say to you, "Fear not, *mon frère,* the tide has turned today—
la liberté
now lights the path,
your sins been washed away."

Walk now, with me
        down *rue de Clichy*
walk now, with me
        down *rue de Clichy*
walk now, with me
        down *rue de Clichy*.

Leave your cares in dat ole world . . .

Come live and be free . . .

David's Letter to Giselle from the Trenches
April 17, 1918

Writing to you is such a pleasant distraction. I have only a couple of nub pencils I keep in my pocket. I trade cigarettes with this gent for these little notebooks, don't ask me where he's getting this nice paper. I'm working on a couple of song ideas. I haven't felt like composing in a long time—nothing like facing death to get you creative, right?

I heard a tiny baby's pitiful cry in a village on our march. Little fella was hungry and his mama was doing her best to console him. She was a young woman who used to be pretty. Her hair was stringy and her dress was worn. We soldiers scrounged up a few *francs* to give her, hope they make it.

So many of these young girls in the countryside are suffering. Sure, you hear that Paris is the City of Light, but these villages bear the heaviest burden of war. Food is short, and stray dogs roam around snapping at us (we almost had to shoot one yesterday).

The Men of Bronze are here because the men from these little towns couldn't cut it, and that's a shame. These are friendly people who love life, love their wine, and love their women. Now, they're at the edge of oblivion.

If any of my fellow soldiers could read these letters, they would never believe they came from me. Except that damned Peyton. He pats me on the back whenever he catches me writing something down as if to say, "Good, good." He thinks he has a way of knowing me, but he doesn't have a clue.

Have to go now, we're on the move.

Yours,
D

Jimmy's Journal
April 17, 1918

I'm not going to lie—it's rough out here, nothing like I ever could have imagined. Everybody deals with it in different ways. Some smoke, some drink, some just kind of check out. The white soldiers keep talking about these poppy plants, but I ain't fooling with that stuff. As for Grenade Tommy, he is a mystery. He talks to himself, I can hear him in between the whistling shells. One thing he shouted really stuck with me, though. He said, "Kraut, the difference between you and me is that you will eventually have to sleep." That's actually kind of true.

I could not have made it this far without David. He's looking out for me, even though he acts like I'm just another one of his soldiers. He's saved my life more than once. One time we were advancing on the field to a new sector of trenches. I was bugling and an Austrian eighty-eight shell was tossed my way and it knocked me to the ground. The wind got knocked out of me and David was the first to get to me. He carried me all the way, under fire, to the medics. I tried to thank him later, but he told me to shut up.

I can get David to talk, sometimes. When we're cleaning our rifles or stitching socks, that's when he'll relax a little and let something slip. I know his father was a ragtime player in New Orleans. He lost his mother about a year ago, and it hurts. I don't know what I'll do if that ever happens to my own Ma. I can't quite tell what the story is about David's brother, though. One time, David said, "He's the best drummer I ever heard."

They're keeping a secret about something bad happened back home. If I ask about that, David just says, "Some dude died, just like every Negro every day in Harlem."

Today he said a curious thing to me.

He said, "Kiddo, I can't like you too much because you could be dead tomorrow."

I feel so honored.

Field Marshall Eric von Helm's Report
to the German High Command
17 April 1918

Morning of 17 April 1918, the Kaiser Battle remains victorious.

Sturmtruppen raids on French trenches continue, high success rate.

Second miscommunication to Gen. Duchene, French Sixth Army, successfully delivered by the asset.

French troops retreating south toward Paris.

Note: Heavy supply shortages and fatigue amongst our soldiers. High outbreaks of influenza. Large number of casualties due to arrival of American divisions.

Repeat: Americans are strengthening the Allies.

David's Letter to Giselle from the Trenches
April 21, 1918

Dearest Giselle,

Thanks for the note, and the treats (I shared the chocolates with Peyton, he was grinning all day). Great to hear your band landed a one-week engagement at the *Opéra de Paris*! I agree that you should put "That Night" into the show—just wait until they find out you are the composer. I am honored that you are dedicating the song to our nightly strolls in Aix-les-Bains.

How am I doing, you ask? It's always the same: Aim. Shoot. Duck. Over and over. It's almost comical how the Germans think that if they tie a twig to the pointy tip of their helmets, that's enough camouflage. I learned that trick from my first battles in the forests with the Legion. I aimed and fired until the bullets ran out. The forest was beautiful, a dark, cool green. With each shot, I let it play out slowly in my mind's eye, the sight of my rifle like the petals of a gunmetal rose unfurling to reveal my target—an eye made of blue ice. There's this split-second recognition of, "Hey, you're the enemy," then it's another split-second of, "I'm going to die." At that moment, he's not just some nameless German—he's somebody else I remember, but I don't talk about that.

I hope to show you my favorite spot in the forest when this is all over. I imagine us in a clearing having a picnic, no war in sight. You would be wearing a red rose behind one ear. That's what I'll think about from now on when I'm firing this rifle.

Another time, another place
would find us laughing
in a field of flowers...

Yours,
D

Giselle's Letter to David
UNDELIVERED
April 21, 1918

I never understood having a passion for anything, until you appeared. I don't remember when it started, but I'm thinking about you all the time, wishing you could hold me like you did the night we were on the dance floor. You grabbed me around the waist and pulled me close... it was so quick, so effortless. I could smell a light musk scent on you from having been under the hot stage lights. Your shirt was smooth, stretching across your strong chest, and I wanted to undo those buttons right there. My heart stopped, then restarted, like a watch having been reset. You pulled me impossibly closer, and we fit so tightly, and the breath left my lungs...

Because of you, I breathe differently now.

I think I'm waiting for you.

But what chance do we have of ever seeing each other again?

Ruth Turner's Letter to David
April 21, 1918

David, I received your letter. "Sorry, Ruth, I can't do this anymore. You deserve a better man." That's all you have to say after all of these years? I have supported your efforts as a musician, stood up for you to my parents, who don't believe that a musician is respectable enough for a debutante.

Why am I not enough for you? You never really gave us a chance, couldn't see what was right in front of you.

I'll admit that you were never completely mine—your restless spirit was always searching for something more, but I was sure that I could get you to focus. Time and again, I find myself waiting for you to finally wake up and see that our lives are passing us by.

You always talk about music, but I've been the one to keep you grounded in reality. Your plans for a band are admirable, but if you don't have a practical purpose for it, how are you going to live? I have enough money for both of us to live comfortably, but I was expecting that we would be married soon. Leaving me behind is a mistake. What are you going to do when you return to the States? I have put money aside to help you get your band started, remember? With my connections, there's nothing you can't do, but you can't do it without me. We've done great things before—remember the orphan benefit concert? The soirees? You can't tell me we're not good together.

Just think some more before you make a rash decision yet again. I'll be here waiting for you to come back to your senses, as always.

Sincerely,
Ruth

Coded Message from Thierry to Giselle
HAND-DELIVERED
21 April 1918

M—

Massive French desertions in St. Mihiel to Verdun.

Hold position and wait for new orders.

From His Imperial Majesty the Kaiser Commander.

For the Fatherland.

—B

Part Three: Men of Bronze

They are possibly the most stoical and mysterious men I've ever known. Nothing surprises them. [M]y boys are public school boys, wise in their day and generation, no caste prejudice, accustomed to the terrible noises of the subway, elevated and street traffic of New York City (which would drive any desert man or Himalaya mountaineer mad) and all are Christians... they have no delusions about the Boche shells coming from any Heathen Gods. They know the d[amned] child-killing Germans are firing at them with pyrocellulose and they know how the breech mechanism works.

—***Letter from Col. Hayward to Emmett Scott***
The American Negro in the World War

David's Notebook in the Trenches
April 22, 1918

Home

We toast bread
on a tiny stove in the back
cozy in this dugout
drinking tea
smoking
inhaling black smoke from exploding Jack Johnsons
reading
writing
        Music.
Hearing that steady beat
        tramp of feet
        grunts of sentry-greeting-sentry
        rifle *tata-tata-tata*
        bullets thudding into mud
        and flesh.

HEADQUARTERS, 369TH INFANTRY
AMERICAN EXPEDITIONARY FORCES

Class one passes attached.

NAME	SERIAL NO	RANK
James Reese Europe	xxxxxxx	1st Lieutenant Regimental Bandleader
Vertner W. Tandy	xxxxxxx	1st Lieutenant, Infantry
David Pierce	xxxxxxx	Corporal Musician 1st Class
James Peyton	xxxxxxx	Corporal Chief Bugler
Percival Fox	xxxxxxx	Specialist Musician 1st Class
Edward Gabriel	xxxxxxx	Private 1st Class Musician 1st Class
Thomas Jones	xxxxxxx	Private 1st Class Musician 1st Class Grenadier*

Jimmy's Letter to His Sister
April 23, 1918

Hi, Sis!

Doing okay, no problems here. Just got granted leave for a while. Looking forward to some good food in the towns. Our canned rations are awful. How are the kids? This war is going to be over soon, I just know it. Getting along fine with all my fellow soldiers here, and David has been so good to me.

And then there's Big Jim. He demands nothing but our best when we perform, and when we fight. If you could just see the intelligence beaming out at you from behind those glasses. He got us here, and he'll get us out. He's got so much in store for us when we return home. A Negro Symphony Orchestra!

Give the kids a hug for me. Tell Ma I'm doing well and she shouldn't worry. I'll be needing that scarf she's knitting for me when I get home.

Much love,
Jimmy

Phil's Letter to David
April 24, 1918

Brother, hope this letter finds you well. Was glad to receive your letter, but are you sure you want to end things with Ruth? She telephoned me once early on, asking how to reach you. I told her I hadn't heard from you since New Year's, when you first got over there. I told her you would be in touch, that we all had to wait for those status cards in the post.

Well, here's my two cents about Ruth. I have been around the block a few times, and I can tell you that she is the cat's pajama's—beautiful and smart, smart enough to know how to build a music business for you. How many times have you talked about putting your own band together? You are good at everything you try. Think about how much more you could do with Ruth behind you.

I didn't agree with you serving in the white man's army, because they don't give a damn about our black asses. But now I see that you're going to return home a war hero. The world will be yours, and Ruth is the right person to share it with.

I put the flowers on Mama's grave for her birthday from us. Stay safe.

Phil

David's Letter to Giselle's Hotel Room in Paris
April 24, 1918

Dearest Giselle,

More agony for me, wondering where you are. This is the only address I have. You have not replied to my last two letters. I'm hearing that there are mass evacuations from towns between "here" and Paris due to the air raids. I hope that you and your band are safe. Do you know how to use a pistol? Please tell me your Frenchy manager knows how to do more in this war than look offended. Can he protect you?

Sorry for the smart remark about Thierry. I'm mad because I don't know what's happening with you...

I have been granted leave from the Front. Peyton, me, and a few other *camerades* will be roaming through some of these small towns for food and drink. I would love to make my way to Paris, but we're ordered not to stray too far, as we might be needed for something big soon.

If only I could hear from you.

Missing you,
D

Jimmy's Journal
April 24, 1918

We got ourselves a good unit: David and me on lead (of course), then there's: Percy Fox, Second Line Eddie Gabriel (more on that later), and Grenade Tommy. I have already picked a name for them—The Terrible Three. Fox is clever and quick on his feet, Eddie calls himself our second line of defense, and Tommy is so good with those grenades, they gave him the rare rank of Grenadier. With grenades you have to be right up on the enemy, with no regard for your own life, so that fits Tommy perfectly. He used to be in a gang back in Harlem, but he got into music and he says it saved his soul. Over here, he gets to make music and blow up everything in sight, the best of both worlds.

Eddie is the newest addition to the team, from another regiment (don't know why), and a surprise to us all. Turns out he and David are cousins on David's father's side. We didn't know until Eddie approached David at rehearsal one day, saying David looked like a dude from a photo back home. Eddie's mother is one of David's aunts from New Orleans. David's face lit up a little when Eddie said he'd learned to play cornet from David's father.

Stupid me, I said, "Hey, maybe you two can work on a tune together, you know, a family reunion?" and David gave me that "Shut the hell up" look, so I knew I had said the wrong thing. I've got to learn not to assume stuff.

David's Letter to Willard from Camp
April 25, 1918

I appreciate being able to write you, because I know you understand. We've been granted about 10 days' leave. I want to see Giselle, but it's not looking likely—she hasn't replied yet. I don't know. My dreams are filled with gunfire and explosions, no rest. I wake up with my pistol in my hand. I had a couple of near misses with Peyton—he needs to stop leaning over me in the trench to check on me. Bullets were whizzing over our heads and he was looking to me to make everything alright. He reminds me of an earlier time in my life that needs to be forgotten, a time when a young man felt like everything would be okay, somehow.

I dread the day Peyton learns the hard lesson about people not giving a damn. I don't want to see that young face crushed. That was my face the day my daddy kicked me in the gut after I travelled all the way down to New Orleans to track his ass down. Mama was down sick, more like sick in the soul, and Phil and I were trying to figure out how to pay the bills because she was not able to work. Mitch loaned me some of his last money and I rode the train down there. I was thinking that if Daddy saw me in the flesh, he couldn't deny me. I was wrong. He was more amazed at my ability to find him than anything else. He kept asking, "Why you here? Why you here?" Last week's shirt was hanging off him, it was dingy and the top button was missing, like somebody had snatched him up. We had heard he was on that junk—I remember him being dark-skinned, but it used to be a smooth ebony, like a polished statue. When I saw him that day, though, he looked like one of those charred corpses from our battlefields. He slurred to me,

"Boy, I don't know why you come down here, but ain't nothing I can do for you. Or your mama. She know I told her to move on, she know that shit. Following me on the road ain't good for a young family." He slowly wagged a trembling finger at me. "You the smart one, boy. You know it was for the best. I can't get no gigs down here anymore, I gotta travel light. I'm goin' north again, but not crowded-ass New York. Naw, Imma check out St. Louis. Just soon as I find some money…"

In the corner was the banged up upright he used to play on, the top missing, the keys brown and chipped. As a child I used to sit on his lap while he played, the smoke from his cigar a sweet smelling haze across my eyes. The tiny black notes were just beyond the mist, just out of my reach. He played Joplin. He played Debussy as well, but that "uppity shit" was played in private. He was a great player, always in high demand at the society balls, cotillions. He wasn't dapper or charming, and he was dark, but he would get the gigs. He got his start playing in brothels as a youth, and, well, that's where his career ended.

He kind of drifted off while talking to me, and I let him. I wanted to study his face while he wasn't moving. But he woke up, still angry I was there. "We free men of color could play anywhere we wanted. Them white folk supported us, then that Plessy Ferguson thing happened and everything changed. We can't play the good places no more. I'm mostly playing in cathouses now. Even them uppity *passé blanc* violin symphony niggers got booted out the concert halls. They cryin' and fiddlin' coon songs now, with me compin'."

His final words to me were, "God, I hope you ain't still playing that cornet I got you."

I stayed with one of his sisters, Aunt Carrie, who was all tearful and sorry and chubby and all she could do was make gumbo for me, full of okra. I hated every slimy bite.

So, Wil, are you an expatriate? Is that who we were back then in the Legion? I never doubted I would return to the States within a year or so—I just needed to get away from there for a while. But you purchased a house here, no regrets. I'm thinking about doing the same thing this time around.

Yours in the Fight,
David

David's Notebook
April 25, 1918

Ragtime's Second Line

Daddy once said,

"Son, one day the Second Line will be swayin' for me,
'erebody wavin' handkerchiefs and pumpin' parasols
like it's the last thing they eva' gonna do on this earth.

We gods
'cause we make folks dance,
but truth is,
our songs are fadin' away.

Promise me you gonna git down low
with that cornet of yours,
front tha line…"

David's Notebook
April 25, 1918

Funeral Rites

A horse drags his dead German rider.
He no longer has a face.
Don't know where they ended up.

Then Mitch appears.
He's shrouded in fire.
Smoke chokes me as I shout his name.

He stands stone-still.
Still dead.
Aneas and Hector reunited in the Underworld.

Except this Hector is not the favorite son of Troy.
Nor Harlem's, for that matter.
His shade haunts the subway now.

David's Letter to Giselle's Hotel Room in Paris
April 25, 1918

Giselle, where are you? I need to hear from you. I get this hollowed-out grinding in my gut, like when I'm out on the battlefield, not knowing what's coming next. I guess you don't have those feelings at all, and I'm just a fool. Maybe you don't have time to miss me when you're with Frenchy. Is that it?

Write me back.

D

Thierry's Note Left for Giselle
April 25, 1918

Liebling:

A reminder that we must remain focused on our work.

I know what is best. Be timely for tonight's show.

Many are counting on us.

Bruno

Giselle's Letter to David
UNDELIVERED
April 25, 1918

Dearest David,

If only you knew how much I miss you, too.

With you, I am a new creation. With him, I am a ghost.

When I'm with him, I pretend he's you.

David's Letter to Giselle from Reims
April 26, 1918

Giselle, I'll continue writing you because it's the only thing I can do. I won't accept that I'll never hear from you again.

We have been granted time off from the trenches. Command is impressed with our progress. The Germans are alarmed by our entrance into this war. *Nous sommes arrivés*! They don't know what to do with us, because "Black don't back down," as we like to say around here. The Germans are calling us "Hellfighters." Some of the guys don't like that name, as we like to call ourselves the Rattlers, but I like both.

We are France's last hope. So many of their soldiers have been killed or have deserted. I don't know much about the English, but I hear things are bad up where they are, too. Death hangs from our shoulders like these heavy, soggy wool coats we wear.

I want you to know everything about me, in case I don't make it. I know that you have secrets you're holding (including your real name), but I choose to believe you have vital reasons. I, on the other hand, want to show you an open ledger.

I recently broke off an engagement to a girl back home. She's the ideal—beauty, good family, well educated. She tries her best to support my music, but she doesn't understand it, not really. Only a fellow artist can understand that chaotic "thing" that drives us to create something out of nothing, the privileged few who are allowed to eavesdrop on God's mind.

This gift comes at a price, though. We give ourselves over to these inspired *communiqués*. As for the people who love us—we're never completely theirs.

It's not that way with you and me.

Please be assured that Ruth and I are over. I am yours.

Yours forever,
D

Jimmy's Journal
April 29, 1918

Sometimes, I can't think too hard about what we're doing here in this war. Are we making things better for the world, or worse? We are answering Germany with better guns and better airplanes, so the ways of killing get better. David and I are staying in this little town outside of Reims, and the folk are just smiling at us, offering us everything they can—bread, apples, wine (which we happily accept). They know the Black Watch is on their side, fighting for them. I'm hoping that America will hear of our good deeds here, but then I get mad at myself for even wanting America's love.

I'll never forget Camp Merritt in New York. Just before we were going to set sail, we were stationed next to a white regiment from Louisiana. They were really cutting up—I think they were trying to bring back the Civil War. A pistol was drawn on one of our men and he was called a son of a bitch of a nigger. We weren't armed, so we borrowed ammo from a white New York regiment (word has it Capt. Ham Fish made it happen for us). Around midnight, I was ordered to sound my bugle, calling the black troops to arms. Capt. Maj. Forbes warned those angry whites that we were also armed and ready to fight back. They stood down, but the bad blood remains. What happens when we see those bastards stateside after this war?

I'm starting to wonder if David is going back home when all of this is over. He is sweet on that Giselle. I think he's now willing to leave his brother behind.

But David and me parting ways after this war?

Unthinkable.

He's always going to need me.

Harlem Journal Interview with Percival "Fox" Fox,
Former "Hellfighter," on the Murder of James Reese Europe
June 1, 1919

[Excerpt reprinted from the May 1919 issue in honor of the late James Reese Europe, as our nation mourns]

by Edwin Moore

PART I

EM: In the wake of the murder of bandleader and war hero James Reese Europe, the world remains stunned at the ironic nature of his death. Tell us your recollections.

Fox: Ironic is the word, alright. To have such a talented, dedicated, and generous person taken from us, just when he was changing the world. He got us respect over there. He was working on creating a Negro National Orchestra here. The doors were opening to us.

EM: When you say "over there," you mean overseas?

Fox: Yes. We were treated like men over there. The French were so appreciative of our help. Their own military had been beaten down so bad, they were deserting all over the place. We come in at the eleventh hour and turn the tide. Big Jim was the first black man to lead troops into combat in this war. If you could have seen him dressed in those shoulder straps and silver bars of a First Lieutenant. When he survived the gas attack that time, that's when we started believing he was more than just a man.

EM: Reports say he cheated death the year before. He was

gassed on patrol duty and barely made it out alive.

Fox: Yeah, my buddy David Pierce got Big Jim out of there. He almost bought it, too.

EM: In our pre-interview conversations, you referred to that "buddy" David. Is he a friend?

Fox: Well, David wasn't exactly the friendly type, but he was the Real McCoy. He was a great musician and a fierce fighter. He was also very experienced, having served before with the French army.

EM: So, David Pierce had previously served in France?

Fox: We never got the whole story, but word is he joined up with Willard Toussaint while in New Orleans. Toussaint was on the boxing circuit and dabbled in vaudeville. He was headed to France to join in on the action, and David went, too. I would have done the same thing. There was nothing for us here, still ain't.

EM: The U.S. Army would not allow Negro men to serve with their fellow Americans in this war.

Fox: Right, that's why we served under the French. We, of all people, believed in freedom—you couldn't find more sincere soldiers... Anyways, well, the world knows about Toussaint—

EM: The stories say he became a flying ace in the Lafayette Escadrille who almost got the Red Baron and shot down a German triplane.

Fox: Right, right. Before that, he and David fought in some of the most deadly battles, including the Battle of Artois Ridge, where he and Toussaint were among the few survivors of hand-to-hand combat.

EM: One would think after surviving that, Pierce would have retired like Toussaint. But instead he came back home to Harlem.

Fox: Yeah, it seems crazy, but I think I know exactly why David re-upped in the service. It was because they killed Mitch.

EM: Mitch? Was he another of your fellow soldiers?

Fox: No, Mitch was a childhood friend of his. I knew Mitch, too. You see, we players all ran in the same circles. We had gigs at the society clubs and the speakeasies, but we knew where our bread was buttered. In the society clubs you entered through the back door, and you didn't mess with the white women. Mitch liked to press his luck. He fell for one of those Miss Annes at a club and they had a thing for a while. Her brother got wind of it, and he put a group together that attacked him and David in the subway after a show. David survived being stabbed, but Mitch didn't. David had just got back stateside. I know that was too much for him, coming back home a man and being told he had to be a boy again...

Willard's Letter to David in Reims
May 5, 1918

Dear Brother-in-Arms,

You did the right thing in reaching out to me. No one understands what is happening better than us. Evil is strangling the hearts of the German people, if only they would realize it. They imagine themselves disrespected, mocked, surrounded by enemies. If only they understood what disrespect really was. They have a weak leader—the Kaiser is just a puppet. There's an icy shadow lurking just behind the throne.

The short answer to your question is yes, I am an expatriate, a man who has abandoned his home country. You're the first person I'm admitting this to. With everyone else, I say it in jest, like, "Oh, I'm only here until the wine dries up, then I'm on the first boat home."

Montmartre is my home now. I'm never going back to the States. Sure, I feel that longing for my birthplace from time to time, but the feeling passes quickly when I remember seeing my father's burned body hanging from that big tree in our front yard. I can still see him swinging like a pendulum, his burnt right ankle twirling counterclockwise, dangling slightly lower than the left. The legs of the new pants that Mama had hemmed for him were singed and melted into his skin. He had gone into town to lease our first tractor. He'd finally saved enough from his work on other people's farms to get his own farm up and running. I guess there were folks who didn't like that idea.

The white men in town who set him afire right in front of us wouldn't let us take him down for two days. We'd wake up in the morning and see him out the kitchen window, all alone out there. And it rained on him. That destroyed my mother. It wasn't too long after that I left home. I fell into the boxing world and didn't look back. Next thing I know I'm over here in the Legion with you. I live here now, and I'll kill every fucking Kraut who dares darken my doorstep.

Make this country your home, too, David. There's nothing for you back there. Your brother will forgive you—he knows why. Get up here in Montmartre as soon as you can, and bring the young Master Peyton and your *chanteuse*. Daisy and I will be waiting for you.

Yours in the Fight,
Wil

Giselle's Letter to David in Reims
May 5, 1918

David, apologies for taking so long to respond. The hotel in Paris forwarded your letters to me. I am happy to know that you are away from the Front. Please tell me you will not have to return there anytime soon. Sorry, but we will not get a chance to see each other in the near future. We were hired to put on some shows in a hospital near Maffrecourt, your base. I had hoped to see you there, but you are far north, and we are not allowed to leave the area due to the increased shelling.

I appreciate your honesty about your woman back home. I am sure that she will continue to wait for you. You deserve a peaceful life after what you have been through. However, I understand your hunger for something more—I feel it, too. You lifted a heavy weight off my soul, but you cannot continue carrying that dark burden.

You talk about what is real, and I, too, have something to say about reality. Not being able to see each other might be a sign. Duty is above everything else. Sometimes, you have to just take what you need to survive and give up what you truly want. No matter how we might feel about one another, perhaps those beautiful moments we shared are all that we should have. Take care, David.

Sincerely,
G

David's Letter to Giselle
May 10, 1918

Giselle, don't be afraid of us. Yes, of course I believe in duty above all else, but I will not accept the idea that I can't have you. There's a world of difference between having what you need and having what you want. I want you.

I still don't know your real name, but I think I have figured out why you chose it. A French soldier here says Giselle means "captive," something about a daughter being promised to a foreign king by her father.

Is that you? I want to be the one who sets you free.

I'll meet you in Paris.

Wait for me.

Yours,
D

Jimmy's Journal
May 11, 1918

Just as we're packing up to hop a train to Paris to find Giselle, we receive new orders.

David is going to kill a lot of Germans.

Capt. Maj. Charles Forbes' Field Notes
May 12, 1918

I will say that our grand experiment with these soldiers is working better than I ever imagined. These are some of the most dedicated and hardworking men I've ever seen. They have such a single-mindedness about this thing, but that's what it will take to win this war.

There are no words for the majestic presence of Lt. Europe. He has such a powerful affect on the men—they would lay down their lives for him, and rightly so. But for all his greatness, I find myself to be continuously intrigued by Cpl. Pierce. Like Europe, Pierce is a fine musician and also possesses that sort of regal air that makes men fall in line behind him. I like how he looks out for his fellow men, especially the young Cpl. Peyton, who worships him.

But there's something else. Pierce has a measured coolness that makes him an excellent shot, an expert at hand-to-hand. There's no more valuable a soldier than one atoning for some past sin—he will march through Hell to get things right this time around.

Pierce and Peyton have received a major assignment, one that may turn the tide of this war. Pierce has been a little unfocused the past few weeks, but today he's thrown himself into his training with a fire in his eyes that I haven't seen since the showdown at Camp Merritt.

I have no doubt that he will succeed in his mission.

Giselle's Letter to David
May 25, 1918

David, I received your note. I am disappointed you cannot join me in Paris, but I take it as another sign we should end things. However, I already know that you will not agree. So, if I cannot convince you to forget about me, we can certainly remain friends. We all need allies in this war, *oui*? I cannot promise you anything else. Let us spend our days writing about what we both love, which is music.

Because of your jazz, I am understanding music in a new way. Our singers are embracing it. One of our best music hall singers, Gaby Deslys, brought a *negre* band here to Paris in a revue just last year, and it was a huge success.

For some of us here, jazz was a threat at first—it is rebellious and disrespectful to tradition. To us *chanson* singers, our old folk songs are comforting, reminding us of family and community. Our operettas charm our audiences, but they can only take us down familiar garden paths. This jazz affects us in ways we cannot understand. *Mon Dieu,* jazz makes us dizzy! It makes us want to dance, even when we are so sad about this war. Jazz seems new to this country, but I am starting to realize it is the oldest song there is, because it is the song of the soul. It is love and pain and all their variations, a symphony of the universe.

You are jazz. *Je suis jazz.*

David's Letter to Giselle
May 25, 1918

Giselle, I will never settle for us being just friends. Did a "friend" make you call out my name in that hotel back in Aix-les-Bains? No. You know what we are to each other, so let's not lose any more time on pretense.

I desperately want to see you, but it turns out I can't join you in Paris. Not yet, but soon. Please don't leave before I get there.

We're back at camp preparing for a big mission that we may not survive. I want to enter into that darkness knowing you'll be waiting for me in the City of Light.

Let me tell what I saw the other day. On our way to this town, we passed by a little church. It was hollowed out by bombs, but it was still standing, somehow. No one will be going out there to pray ever again—the landmines took care of that. We had a soldier leading us past the church with a metal detector—poor fool had lost a bet, so it was his job for the day. He was sweating a river.

As we made our way through there, a little bird swooped in and landed on top of the empty doorframe. We watched each other as I carefully passed by. We wanted to ask each other the same thing:

What are you doing here?

I thought about the grand ceremony that was waiting for me back home, and God as my witness, I didn't want any of that—the bridesmaids, the groomsmen, the flowers, the ribbons, all the things she went on about. I didn't give a damn if Auntie Evelyn or Auntie Pauline wanted to sing at the wedding—neither one of them could hold a note if their lives depended on it.

I owed Ruth a wedding, though. It's what you do when you have a great gal with so much to offer, right? Especially when she knows you're still a work in progress, yet she's willing to work you up. She was going to make a better man out of me. But there I was, standing in that bombed-out sanctuary imagining a wedding with you instead.

Let's get to that church someday—just you, me, and that little blue bird. Maybe God will choose to return by then. You and I will hold hands, and our vows will come straight from our hearts. I bet the war will even pause for this union of two souls who found each other across the ocean. Your love called me forth from a cold, muddy trench. You are my resurrection. You make me want to write songs again.

Oui, nous sommes jazz...
We are jazz, and just as timeless...

David's Notebook
May 25, 1918

Supposin'
(Ragtime Love in Bloom)

Su-pposin'...
a gal like you
walks up to a guy like me?

Su-pposin'...
a guy like me
then drops on bended knee?

Su-pposin'...
this lovely gal says,

"I do" to me?

Su-pposin'
you did...

Su-pposin'
I did...

Let's wed right under this tree...

Thierry's Note Left for Giselle at Rehearsal
May 26, 1918

Liebling:

We will meet at the rendezvous point.

Our allies in Chateau-Thierry are prepared to greet our "friends"—your false intel was successfully transmitted.

You do not seem yourself as of late. You are hereby ordered to keep all relations with that cornet player professional only. You have achieved your goal of earning his trust. It is now time to regain your focus. He has even had a bad influence on your songwriting—what is this jazz music?

You and I have been serving together for a long time, and I see a future for us beyond this "tour," which will be coming to an end very soon. I will discuss this matter with you after the mission is completed.

Bruno

Excerpt from Cable from the Western Front
to the Harlem Journal
26 May 1918

A Special Report on "Our Fighting 369th"
from the French Battlefields:
The Battle of Henry Johnson
Edwin Moore, Reporting

The 15th New York Infantry is now known not only for its exceptional regimental band's music under maestro Lt. James Reese Europe, but for its bravery. Early on the morning of May 14, 1918, a German patrol of at least two-dozen soldiers attacked Combat Group Number 29, a small post manned by only five men. With their corporal and two men trapped inside a dugout with no means of escape, two privates who had been on guard duty—Needham Roberts from Trenton, NJ and Henry Johnson from Albany, NY—jumped into action. Though vastly outnumbered and wounded by grenades, Roberts and Johnson fought back like wild tigers, killing at least four of the German attackers, wounding many others, and forcing the rest to retreat. Low on ammunition and Roberts nearly unconscious, Johnson used his rifle as a club and his eight-inch bolo knife. . .

From Noble Sissle's Broadway Notebook

May 1920

[Draft lyrics for Hero Henry part from *Hero of No Man's Land* musical]

<u>Intro</u>

I pulled a gun to make him stay, that white lieutenant.
The pride of America, he was gonna abandon his men.

Chorus: *Say it ain't so, Henry!*

They keep tryin' to arrest me, 'cause my "swelled head" is making me talk too much. But no jail can hold my truth.

Chorus: *You tell 'em, Henry!*

Marines behind the lines didn't want us there.
They attacked us as bad as the Germans.

Chorus: *Say it ain't so, Henry!*

They keep tryin' to take my uniform, the one I wore so proud in France. But no naked shame will cover my truth.

[Hero Henry salutes, eyes straight ahead]

Chorus: *You tell 'em, Henry!*

Chorus: *Henry! The Hero of No Man's Land,*

the one man

who can

heal our land.

From Noble Sissle's Broadway Notebook
May 1920

[Notes for *Hero of No Man's Land*]

Henry Johnson's postwar speaking tour is starting to make people uncomfortable. The white audiences don't want to hear the truth. The military is trying to have him arrested.

Henry Johnson Quotes:
"The war was won by black soldiers."

"I did it because it was my duty. I did it for Albany. That's what I went for."

"One officer said, 'send the niggers to the front and there won't be so many around New York.'"

"They may put the Negroes in the rear seats of cars here, but they did not make any discrimination in No Man's Land."

Argus Age Editorial:
The greatest individual hero produced by the whole American army

should

Stay off the lecture platform.

Excerpt from the Harlem Journal
July 10, 1929

THE DEATH OF HENRY JOHNSON
by Edwin Moore

The 15th New York Infantry has lost its greatest hero. After nearly ten years out of the public eye, war hero Henry Johnson of Albany, New York died on July 1 in poverty. Johnson, a former railcar porter, distinguished himself in battle as a member of the 369th Infantry. He earned the nickname "Black Death." Decorated with France's highest honor, the Croix de Guerre, Johnson was buried with full military honors at Arlington National Cemetery. . .

Field Marshall Eric von Helm's Report
to the German High Command
27 May 1918

FIELD MARSHALL REPORT

Morning of 27 May 1918, the Kaiser's Battle began 4,000 gun bombardment of the Allies. Heavy losses to the British.

Gen. Duchene, French Sixth Army, defied orders from French Commander-in-chief Petain to abandon Chemin des Dames Ridge despite German capture a year prior.

Miscommunication to Duchene successfully delivered by the asset.

Bombardment was followed by poison gas drop. After gas lifted, main infantry assault by 17 Sturmtruppen divisions.

German army advancement through Allied lines. Eight Allied divisions smashed between Reims and Soissons. Aisne was taken in under six hours.

Over 50,000 Allies and 800 guns captured.

Note: Heavy supply shortages. Heavy soldier fatigue. Heavy casualties from Allied counterattacks.

Repeat: Allies launching strong counterattacks.

Jimmy's Journal
May 28, 1918

The band has been playing a lot of funerals lately for the soldiers killed at the Front. At first it was just French and Germans, but now it's Americans, too. More and more small wooden crosses. We play "Flee as a Bird," a traditional hymn. When Big Jim's serving with Command, Noble Sissle, his right-hand man (excellent violinist) takes over with the band, along with Sgt. Mihell, but everyone understands this is Jim's band. If we play for the locals or French troops, or visiting high officials, we might also play some plantation melodies—Sissle does a nice vocal on Foster's "Old Folks at Home," accompanied by a trombone for an organ-like effect. It soars with a crescendo of horns, cymbals, and drums. They always request "Memphis Blues," though—Big Jim originally thought audiences wouldn't take to it because it's a little slower than the dance tunes, but now it's one of our hits.

They're preparing us for a raid across no-man's-land. This time, Big Jim is leading the charge. David told Capt. Forbes that Big Jim shouldn't be put in unnecessary danger, as he's too important. Capt. Forbes agrees, but it's already been cleared between the French command and the Colonel. The best he could do, Forbes said, was to send David and us along to watch over Big Jim. This might be my greatest mission.

Coded Message Hand-Delivered
to Giselle's Dressing Room
1 June 1918

M—

Massive French desertions. We have arrived at outpost near Chateau-Thierry, less than 50 miles from Paris. Victory is imminent. Unit awaiting your arrival.

For the Fatherland.

—B

Harlem Journal Interview with Percival "Fox" Fox,
former "Hellfighter"

[Excerpt reprinted from the April 1919 issue in honor of the Late James Reese Europe, as our nation mourns the loss of the great bandleader]

by Edwin Moore

Part II

EM: After spending so much time making music here and then serving with him in France, did you gain any insights into the musical mind of Mr. Europe?

Fox: Well, I would say it's more about me being a witness to genius. Jim put it real simple in a newspaper interview one time. He said, "A new type of Negro musician has appeared." He rearranged the orchestra, added the saxophone yet giving it a muted sound that didn't overwhelm things. Suddenly, the drummer was the star. The drum set was expanded to include wood blocks, bells, cymbals, triangles, and marching band drums like the bass and snare, and they were controlled by one drummer like back in the vaudeville days. Jim's orchestra alone was worth the price of admission—his development of the rhythm section as the centerpiece was unprecedented. Then there's the work Big Jim did with the Castles. Here you had a white man and woman dancing to a new form of music created by a black man, with an all-black orchestra dressed in tuxedos. You can't top that.

EM: It is indeed a new musical era in America.

Fox: People didn't know what to call this music at first, all they could do was dance to it. At one show, Jim was directing three different orchestras, accompanying a 25-member dance chorus, all at once. The Castles were one of a kind—Irene was the new woman of the century—stylish, daring, sexy. They were breaking box office records and a dance craze was born. Oh my, the dancing! The glorious foxtrot—you're gliding or sliding in two slow steps, then hopping and kicking in four... So many other bandleaders are now following Jim's lead with that syncopated dance music. The Castle Tour was a high-point for sure, until the Hellfighters started doing their thing in France, that is. Just look at his legacy. Who knows what's next? It's certainly going to be great.

EM: So, has Mr. Europe shared with the band what's coming next? Can you share any secrets with our readers?

Fox: No secrets here, I'm happy to tell you that plans are in the works for a Negro Symphony Orchestra. I can't wait. I thank God every day that Corporal David Pierce was there to save Big Jim from that gas attack last June...

Article from the Harlem Journal
June 15, 1918

HARLEM HELLFIGHTERS RECEIVE BATTLEFIELD PROMOTION

by Edwin Moore

In what can only be described as the greatest act of heroism this side of the Battle of Henry Johnson, the actions of Corporals David Pierce and James Peyton has secured a place for "Harlem's Own" in American history. Thanks to the swift actions of Pierce and Peyton, now affectionately known and "PNP" (a là "TNT"), American Treasure Lieutenant James Reese Europe lives to compose another day. In a bitter battle to secure a French outpost under attack by the Germans, Lt. Europe was pinned down by the enemy. PNP rushed in to save him, supported by their three fellow soldiers, Percival Fox, Thomas Jones, and Edward Gabriel, known as "The Terrible Three." Unbeknownst to them at the time, poison gas was left behind by the Germans. With quick thinking and without regard for their own lives, PNP managed to save Lt. Europe from the worst of the gas. Due to Lt. Europe's bedside testimony, Corporals Pierce and Peyton have been given rare battlefield promotions to Sergeant.

Pierce was reportedly reluctant to receive the honor, but did so at the urging of his comrade, Sergeant Peyton.

"I only did what any of us in the Old 15th New York would have done," Pierce said.

David's Letter to Willard
Field Hospital No. 129
June 15, 1918

First thing is, I'm okay. No words for what happened, but this needs to be put down so I can prove to myself that it was real.

Our mission was tough, support for a strategic post that was failing. We lost some men, mostly French, but we lost one of our guys, Pvt. Ramirez. He was a fine drummer. He had children down in Puerto Rico, where Jim recruited him. He had invited us down there after the war, we were going to drink rum together.

When we arrived at the trench near Chateau-Thierry, it was chaos. We entered through an opening where the Germans had cut through the barbed wire and rolled it aside. With a width of about four men, the trench seemed to be the most deeply dug one that I ever had the displeasure of entering. I don't know. As we looked down inside, we saw blood-covered blue uniforms scattered to and fro. That outpost was already lost—it was a trap.

Rightly so, Big Jim slowed our advance down into the trench. He stopped some men on the ladders. It was too quiet—there should have been somebody rattling something around down there. We knew the attackers hadn't left yet—we would have seen them running across no-man's-land, which was wide open before us. Rifles and blades drawn, we completed the drop then walked as quietly as we could across the wooden plank floors. Around the first corner, we heard a small creak in the floor.

Out jumped a raiding party of Germans, four men wide and countless deep. We were outnumbered. Big Jim yelled for us to get back above ground. We ran, the Germans on our heels. When we got back to the entrance, we scrambled up the pair of ladders we'd just descended. Peyton was ahead of me and I shouted to him to move his ass. He got out. As I was scrambling over the top, I heard a curse from Ramirez, who was behind me, then a thump. I turned to see that soldier being pulled down. I tried to grab him, but I wasn't fast enough. They proceeded to gut him open with their knives right there. That was the fastest I ever climbed a ladder—I practically leaped out of there. Back above ground, I took several stumbling steps backward, waiting for them. As they approached the top, one of theirs used the top of another ladder to shoot cover, careful not to hit his comrades as they climbed up the first ladder and out. Once above ground, everyone scattered. If only we'd been able to climb out and turn around fast enough to rain fire down into that hellhole—they would have died like rats in a barrel.

Despite the horror of what was happening, nothing has—or ever shall—shake me the way I was shaken when I recognized one of the soldiers climbing out of that pit.

It was Giselle.

My Giselle.

She was with the Germans. She's in with those demons.

She was wearing a German uniform, helmet, boots and all. Once she got above ground, she rushed a French soldier from behind—I was too shocked to warn him. Peyton and Fox saw everything, too. Everything. Once the French soldier was down, Giselle shot him in the face. Then she was just gone.

Fox was yelling at us to get Big Jim. Time sped back up. I turned and saw Jim just beyond me to my left. He was on the ground. Above him, a German was swinging downward with a long blade. I jumped into action, but I couldn't feel my legs.

Racing to get there in time, I saw Peyton from the corner of my eye. He was coming from the other side, his face twisted with rage. I never want to see him that way ever again. Once I got to Jim, I pulled the German away with everything I had left in me. I slammed him to the ground and onto his back. He looked so surprised—I'll always wonder if it was because of my brown face. Peyton and I pounced on him like wild animals. I pulled out my blade and stabbed him right in the heart. Blood spurted in our faces then swelled out of him like a fountain. I don't know if that man had a family or not, but that was the one time I didn't care.

Just as we were pulling Jim to his feet, we found ourselves surrounded by a strange flickering haze. My face felt flushed, and my nose was burning. There was this loud hissing sound—I was surprised I could hear anything over all the other noise. I then saw the canister rolling past Jim's boots. Fox was still running toward us, but his eyes were wide. The Germans took off—they knew what they had just unleashed.

Fox was yelling "Gas!"and waving us off. We hauled Jim, who was stunned, away from the gas. Every second felt like a year. We reached an incline and rushed up onto a little grassy mound where we dropped to our knees. I remember my chest burning, then everything went black.

I woke up here in the hospital later that morning.

Peyton is okay. Big Jim is alive, so I am grateful.

I don't know what happened to Giselle, but I know that she is alive. I can still feel her.

Wil, I want to take you up on the offer to visit when they let me out of here. I need to regroup.

Then I'm going after her.

Preach's Sermon Notes
June 15, 1918

The Lord is with us, always.

He sends us signs and wonders. Remember that even in this most evil of wars, He sent a vision of St. Michael the Archangel to Mons last year so that the French soldiers could be inspired. Remember the Golden Virgin—Mother and Child are still dangling on top of that ruined basilica in Albert.

The story goes, whichever side brings the statue down is destined to lose the war…

Phil's Letter to David at the Base

June 15, 1918

Brother, I haven't heard anything else from you since your letter in April, so I'm writing to your last known location. I have some news that I believe will change your mind about staying over there. I know I was a big part of that decision, and I don't blame you. However, here's a very good reason for you to return home:

Ruth telephoned. She is expecting, about six months along.

She says when she received your breakup letter it was a shock, so she regrets her angry reply. She figured you would be coming home soon anyway, and she'd just surprise you with the news then. (Some of us predicted you brothers would wash out and be sent back home pretty quick, but I guess not.) Ruth had no doubt her news would change everything, and you would be pleased. But she says you haven't been answering her letters since—I don't believe that.

She couldn't reach me for a good while either. I've been on the run these past several months, trying to get something going down in New Orleans. I'm feeling the pull to our real home, you know? Been feeling this strong connection to Daddy. I want to know who he really was, before he gave up. I'm playing in some of his old haunts—I'll fill you in on that part later, but I talked to somebody who played with Daddy just before he disappeared.

You can imagine the embarrassment for Ruth's parents about the baby, their perfect daughter and all, so they sent her to stay with relatives in D.C. until your child is born. They had convinced Ruth to forget about you and raise the child on her own, but she wants you in your child's life. I don't even have to guess if you knew about the baby or not—you would have done right by them if you had known. Now's your chance.

I went to see her, and she's doing well. She asked me to reach out to you, so that's what I'm doing. You have a chance to be the father you never had. I should have been a father to you, but I failed you and corrupted you. If you hadn't helped me in that alley before the police came, I would be in prison right now. You worked any job you could find when Mama was down, and I should have been doing the same.

The least I can do is give you some fatherly advice now. Come back home, marry Ruth, and build a life for yourself. Those French people are loving you all right now, but when this war ends they will be kicking you out. This, I know.

You can find a way to love Ruth the way you think you love that singer. Worldly women like her will only break your heart. Coming home to Ruth and your child will give you a sure thing.

God certainly steps in sometimes, doesn't He?

Phil

The Remembrance Saga continues...

REMEMBRANCE, BOOK TWO: **VICTORS** (2017)

REMEMBRANCE, BOOK THREE: **EMPIRE** (2018)

REMEMBRANCE, BOOK FOUR: **BRAVE NEW WORLD** (2019)

Acknowledgments

There are too many wonderful people and institutions to thank for their assistance, but I must mention some who were critical to the creation of this book and The Remembrance Project. Thank you to Reginald Flood and Brian Gilmore for their support above and beyond this project; thanks always to Randall Horton, my partner—we have built new worlds for our people, together. Thank you to these poets and writers: Derrick Harriell, whose pioneering, multidimensional work, *ROPES*, showed me what was possible; Curtis L. Crisler, whose every work demonstrates musicality in its purest form; Angie Chuang, for living a life dedicated to the pursuit of truth and understanding; Antoinette Gardner, an angel of mercy. Thank you to these exemplary musicians: composer and bandleader Tracy Kash; composer Matthew Raetzel and musician and director Arthur Ray, who brings my creative visions to life with such grace and excellence. Thank you to Ron English, Detroit's musical treasure; composer T.J. Anderson, whose musical excellence is inspiring, and most importantly, Mircea Cure, my teacher and friend. A special thanks to E.B. the cornet player—you are love and magic.

Thank you to my family for everything, especially my parents, sisters, nephews, niece, cousins, and "big" brother, Gerald. This book is for my father, a brave veteran of Vietnam and for my uncles and cousins in the military, especially my uncles George, Fendrick, and Edward, unsung soldiers who served in post-WWII America, Korea, and Vietnam. Every book is dedicated to my mother, who taught me to read and who told me that I was a writer.

Special thanks to The Write Now critique group in Detroit for so many great years of friendship and writing; Susannah Cleveland, head of the BGSU Music Library and Sound Recording Archives; Vincent Livoti, Palmer School of Library & Information Science, Long Island University, and the Schomburg Center for Research in Black Culture, NYC.

As always, thank you to the 369th, past and present, and all African Americans "in the service" who sacrifice so much in the name of freedom.

About the Author

H. Buchanan is a writer and multimedia producer. Her work appears in print and digital publications, including *MÖBIUS, The Blood Jet Writing Hour* and *Look At Flatbush,* where she is a contributing editor. A musician, Buchanan is a member of the Society for American Music. She is the executive producer of *The Remembrance Project,* a centennial print, digital, and musical tribute to the Harlem Hellfighters.

CPSIA information can be obtained
at www.ICGtesting.com
Printed in the USA
LVOW11s2224281016
510741LV00001B/1/P